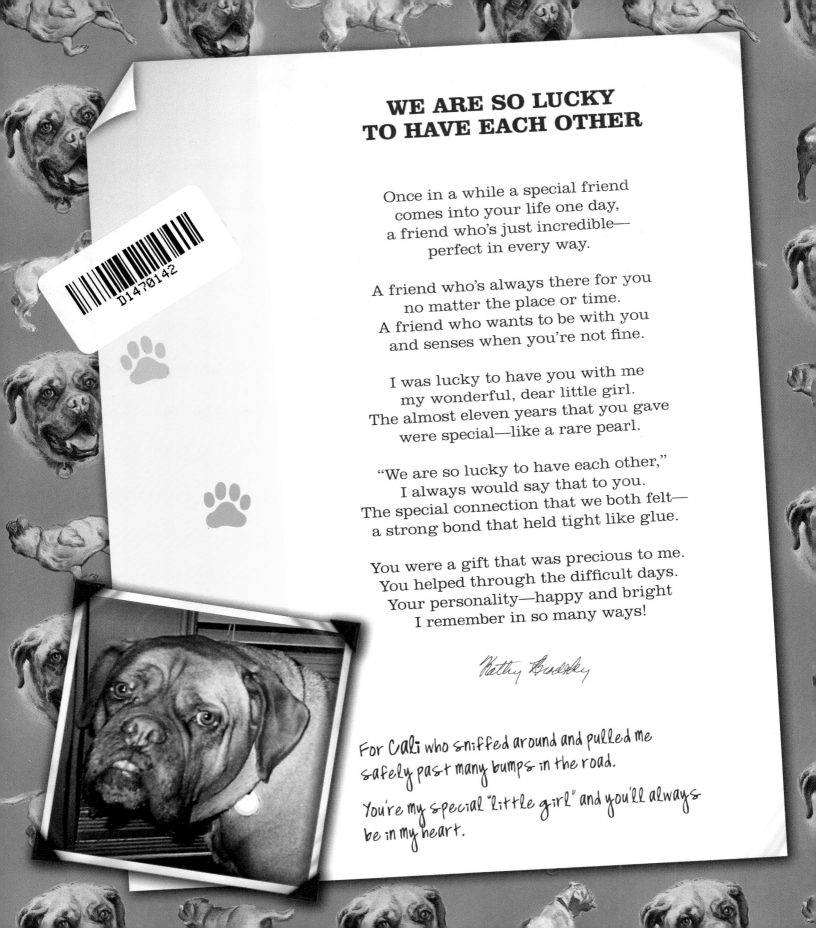

# WE ARE SO LUCKY
# TO HAVE EACH OTHER

Once in a while a special friend
comes into your life one day,
a friend who's just incredible—
perfect in every way.

A friend who's always there for you
no matter the place or time.
A friend who wants to be with you
and senses when you're not fine.

I was lucky to have you with me
my wonderful, dear little girl.
The almost eleven years that you gave
were special—like a rare pearl.

"We are so lucky to have each other,"
I always would say that to you.
The special connection that we both felt—
a strong bond that held tight like glue.

You were a gift that was precious to me.
You helped through the difficult days.
Your personality—happy and bright
I remember in so many ways!

*Kathy Budesky*

For Cali who sniffed around and pulled me
safely past many bumps in the road.

You're my special "little girl" and you'll always
be in my heart.

# just sniffing around

To Connor, Clio & Wyatt —
Your Grandpa
knew you'd
have fun reading
this "little" Dog Book!
Kathy Brodsky

**By Kathy Brodsky**

Illustrations by
**Cameron Bennett**

I'm a very special dog!
They tell me every day.

I'm always ready for some fun.
I love to run and play.

Sometimes they get mad at me.

I didn't do a thing!

I just chewed up a little shoe
and buried a sparkly ring!

I have good ears; I hear it all.
When someone's at the door

I bark and bark to let them know.
My job is not a bore.

When no one's home, I'm on the couch.
**My secret's safe with me.**

I hear them come, then jump and run
**to greet them happily!**

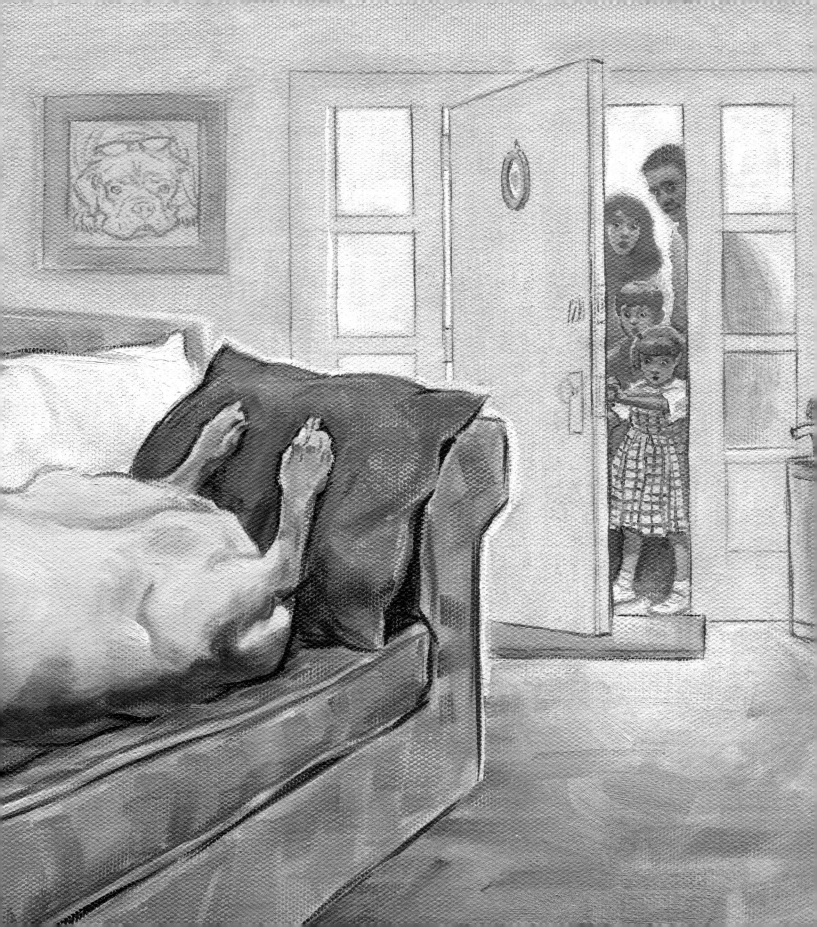

Every day when we go out
**I walk them all around.**

I hate it when they jerk my neck!
**I love to sniff the ground.**

Sniffing is a special skill
that tells me many things.

I always find my hidden bones...
Where did I hide that ring?

Who's that strutting over there?
A new face on the street.

Here she comes to have some fun.

I'm up and on my feet!

I'm always ready for a ride...
See me here zooming past.

I stick my head out all the way.
It really is a blast!

I hear the rustling of food.
I hurry, then I wait.

A little drool may start to drip...
Give me what's on YOUR plate!

Doggy daycare here I come!

I play with friends all day.

But when I sleep there overnight
I wish my folks could stay.

They said that very yucky word—
"The VET!" That's what I heard.

I wish that I could fly away...

Too bad I'm not a bird.

My family plays ball with me
in our park down the street.

They throw the ball, I run for it,
**then drop it at their feet.**

Sometimes I try to steal the ball.
They yell, "HEY! That's NOT RIGHT!"

I hold it tight and run and run
'til they're nowhere in sight.

Then I'm scared because I'm lost.
**Where is my family?**

I see them now, near that bent tree.
I run; they run to me!

Safe at home with everyone—
**so glad I'm not alone.**

I snuggle with my family.
Hey, LOOK! A brand new bone.

That's my doggy life, "WOOF! WOOF!"
I'm such a lucky pooch.

HOORAY! I see a friendly face.
It needs a BIG WET SMOOCH!

# DIGGING FURTHER...

**1** The American Kennel Club (AKC) registers purebred dogs and separates them into eight different groups. Do you know that the dogs in each group are bred for different purposes? Can you learn the names of the groups and find out what breeds are in each?

**2** If your dog is purebred, is it listed in the AKC dog grouping, or in another kennel club? If your dog is in one of the dog groups, is it registered? Where would you find more information?

**3** Dogs can be trained to help people in a variety of ways. How are dogs chosen for special training and how old are they when they begin?

You might be surprised to learn who some trainers are and where the dogs are trained.

**4** Dogs have helped people for thousands of years and continue to do so in many ways. How do dogs help people with physical or mental disabilities and/or medical problems?

**5** How can dogs be used in law enforcement and search and rescue missions? Do you know how dogs help farmers?

**6** How can your dog learn to be a Certified Therapy Dog who is specially trained to visit schools, hospitals, nursing homes, etc? Wouldn't it be fun to bring cheer to others as you and your tail-wagging friend work as a team?

**7** Can you think of other ways that dogs help people?

**1** What's your dog's name? Who named your dog and how old is your furry friend? How long are dog years compared to human years? Is your dog a purebred or mixed breed?

**2** Where did you get your dog and how old was your dog when she or he came to live with you?

**3** Why is it important to spay or neuter a pet? Was your dog spayed or neutered? Has your dog had puppies? What was that like and where are the puppies now?

**4** How many pets do you have? Does your dog play with cats or with other animal friends? Who takes care of your dog (feeding, walking, grooming)?

**5** Where does your dog stay during the day and where does your dog sleep at night? What's your dog's regular routine? Does your dog have favorite things he or she does—any tricks? What games do you play with your dog? What are your dog's travel experiences?

**6** If your dog had a party, who would he or she invite and why? What foods would be served? Would you like to have a party for your dog?

**7** Has your dog had obedience lessons? Who helped train your dog and how do you handle any bad habits your dog may have? How should you approach a dog you don't know?

**8** When was the last time your dog went to the vet? What was the purpose of the visit? Has your dog ever been sick? What happened? Have you ever had a dog die? What was that like for you?

**9** How can you tell if your dog is happy or sad? If your dog could talk, what would he or she tell you?

**10** How would your dog describe you? Do you ever tell your dog things you wouldn't tell anyone else? Does your dog understand?

**11** What would your life be like if you didn't have a dog?

# just sniffing around

**J**ust Sniffing Around was inspired by all of the dogs I've owned or known. Any dog lover will agree that the scenes in the book, so wonderfully illustrated by Cameron Bennett, represent the qualities that endear these special four-legged friends to our hearts.

My dog Cali is the star of the book. She was the most incredible dog—a real "people person" who was always looking to welcome someone—in our home or on the street. When we were out for a walk, Cali would often sit and wait to greet people she saw two blocks away. It didn't matter to her whether she knew them or not; she loved everyone and everyone loved her. She brought her smile and her wagging tail to many.

Cali actually helped me start writing picture books! Several years ago, while taking our usual walk, I noticed a pine tree that was crooked. That discovery inspired me to write a poem which became the book *My Bent Tree*. Cali was also there for every moment of *The Inside Story*.

Unfortunately, Cali developed bone cancer in August, 2008. Even though we did everything we could to help her live as pain-free as possible, in early December that year, a month shy of her eleventh birthday, Cali died peacefully in her sleep. It was a huge loss for all of us. Most of the time, large breed dogs have a shorter life span than smaller ones.

I wanted to write a book about dogs in general, but also to write something special for Cali. She was a French Mastiff, a Dogue de Bordeaux. This breed became a member of the Working Class Group of the American Kennel Club in 2008.

No matter what size, shape, or color our dogs are, we're lucky that they share their lives with us! I'm sure some of the scenes in *Just Sniffing Around* remind you of your special dogs.

*Kathy Brodsky*

*Just Sniffing Around* is for dog lovers of any age. For more information about my other books, please visit my website **www.helpingwords.com**

Many people contributed to *Just Sniffing Around* in countless ways. Some helped even before the book was written. Special thanks to Cameron; Julia; Greg; Jeff; Karen and the Pet-Agree staff; Kathy and the Holistic Veterinary staff; Barb and the Daniel Webster Animal staff ; Anna and Steve of Charles River Dogue de Bordeaux; Louise; Mary; the Spencer family; and Kim and Aaron at wedü.

Also, thanks to everyone who listened, looked, and gave advice. I appreciate your input and enthusiasm.

# Thank you all!

Publisher's Cataloging-in-Publication
(Provided by Quality Books, Inc.)

Brodsky, Kathy.
   Just sniffing around / by Kathy Brodsky ; art by Cameron Bennett.
   p. cm.
   SUMMARY: This rhyming story follows the daily life of one dog as a way to present the little quirks and personalities that endear dogs to people. Includes discussion questions about dogs in general, as well as questions for thinking about one's own pet.
   ISBN-13: 978-0-578-03620-5
   ISBN-10: 0-578-03620-7

   1. Dogs--Juvenile fiction.  2. Human-animal relationships--Juvenile fiction.  [1. Dogs--Fiction. 2. Human-animal relationships--Fiction.  3. Pets--Fiction. 4. Stories in rhyme.]   I. Bennett, Cameron (Cameron D.), ill.  II. Title.

PZ8.3.B782Jus 2010      [Fic]
      QBI09-600136

Published by Helpingwords
Just Sniffing Around © 2010
Printed in the U.S.A.
Printed on recycled paper

Kathy Brodsky
helpingwords.com
66 Prospect Street
Manchester, NH 03104
ISBN-13: 978-0-578-03620-5